my itty-bitty bio

Coco Gauff

CHERRY LAKE PRESS

Published in the United States of America by Cherry Lake Publishing
Ann Arbor, Michigan
www.cherrylakepublishing.com

Reading Adviser: Marla Conn, MS, Ed., Literacy specialist, Read-Ability, Inc.
Book Designer: Jennifer Wahi
Illustrator: Jeff Bane

Photo Credits: © Thierrydehove/Dreamstime.com, 5; © pisitnamtasaeng/Shutterstock, 7; © Rosshelen/Dreamstime.com, 9; © Neale Cousland/Shutterstock, 11; © Zhukovsky/Dreamstime.com, 13, 22; © Leonard Zhukovsky/Shutterstock, 15, 23; © lev radin/Shutterstock, 17, 19; © Rena Schild/Shutterstock, 21; Cover, 1, 6, 10, 16, Jeff Bane; Various frames throughout, © Shutterstock images

Cherry Lake Press is an imprint of Cherry Lake Publishing Group.

Library of Congress Cataloging-in-Publication Data

Names: Pincus, Meeg, author. | Bane, Jeff, 1957- illustrator.
Title: Coco Gauff / Meeg Pincus ; illustrated by Jeff Bane.
Description: Ann Arbor, Michigan : Cherry Lake Publishing, 2021. | Series: My itty-bitty bio | Includes index. | Audience: Grades K-1
Identifiers: LCCN 2020005655 (print) | LCCN 2020005656 (ebook) | ISBN 9781534168398 (hardcover) | ISBN 9781534170070 (paperback) | ISBN 9781534171916 (pdf) | ISBN 9781534173750 (ebook)
Subjects: LCSH: Gauff, Coco, 2004- | Women tennis players--United States--Biography--Juvenile literature. | Tennis players--United States--Biography--Juvenile literature.
Classification: LCC GV994.G38 P56 2021 (print) | LCC GV994.G38 (ebook) | DDC 796.342092/52--dc23
LC record available at https://lccn.loc.gov/2020005655
LC ebook record available at https://lccn.loc.gov/2020005656

Printed in the United States of America
Corporate Graphics

table of contents

About the author: Meeg Pincus has been a writer, editor, and educator for 25 years. She loves to write inspiring stories for kids about people, animals, and our planet. She lives near San Diego, California, where she enjoys the beach, reading, singing, and her family.

About the illustrator: Jeff Bane and his two business partners own a studio along the American River in Folsom, California, home of the 1849 Gold Rush. When Jeff's not sketching or illustrating for clients, he's either swimming or kayaking in the river to relax.

my story

I was born in Florida. It was 2004. I have two younger brothers.

My mom and dad were **athletes**. I tried many sports as a child. I loved tennis most.

What do you love to do?

My dad coaches me. My mom **homeschools** me. My parents **sacrificed** a lot to support my tennis playing.

I **admired** Serena and Venus Williams. They **inspired** me.

Who do you admire?

I was the youngest girl ever to play in the junior **U.S. Open** finals. I was 13.

I beat Venus Williams in a match! I was 15. I thanked her for being a **role model**.

I want to be a tennis champion. This means that I train hard. I **focus**. I don't quit.

My parents taught me to have a good **attitude**. I've learned to stay calm during hard matches.

How do you stay calm?

I am chasing my goal. I work hard. I want to be a role model for other tennis players.

What would you like to ask me?

2017

2000

Born
2004

2019

2100

glossary & index

glossary

admired (ad-MIRED) looked up to someone

athletes (ATH-leets) people who are trained in or very good at sports and physical exercise

attitude (AT-ih-tood) your opinions and feelings about something that affect how you behave

focus (FOH-kuhs) to concentrate

homeschools (HOME-skoolz) teaches someone at home or somewhere else outside of a school

inspired (in-SPIRED) filled with a feeling or idea

role model (ROHL MAH-duhl) a person whose behavior is imitated by others

sacrificed (SAK-ruh-fised) gave up something for the sake of something or someone else

U.S. Open (YOO ES OH-puhn) an important contest held in the United States that draws tennis players from around the world

index